By Laura Langston • Illustrated by Lindsey Gardiner

Remember, Grandma?

VIKING

My grandma lives with us now because she can't remember.
She is not the wrinkled kind; she's the special
kind instead. She wears high-top sneakers with
yellow laces and she laughs very loud.
Once she had a houseboat and an art gallery by
the sea. Then she played the piano and
made mile-high apple pie.

Now
she sits in
her special chair
and rocks quick,
quick,
quick.

Dad says that one day Grandma's remembering will go away forever.

She will forget everything, even our names. He is wrong.

Grandma still reads me stories,

only now I help her with the words.

We still go outside to play, and Grandma still talks to the birds.

We **giggle** and **laugh** and **sing** special songs together.

When Grandma gets **mixed** up, I tell her it's time for a nap.
I keep her company while she rests.

Some days, Grandma jumps when her very own cat lands on her lap.
"And **Who** are **yOu**?" she asks.

"That's Princess Pepper," I say. "She loves you very much."
I feed the cat and comb the tangles out of her fur.

She keeps my
grandma warm.

After school, I practice the piano. Sometimes Grandma
nods her head and doesn't say anything at all.
Other times she tells me how well *I* have done.

"Excellent, Margaret,"
she says. "Chopin
would be proud."

I give her a hug. I was playing Bach,
but Grandma can't remember.

Grandma still plants sweet peas
in the spring.

"They are the only flower worth growing,"
she says, "because they smell so wonderful."

The flowers grow **tall** and **pretty**. I cut a huge handful and bring them inside. I put them under Grandma's nose. "Smell."

"**Lovely**," she says. "Roses are my favorite flower."

She rocks her chair quick, quick, quick. Princess Pepper jumps down.

"It's okay," Mom whispers when she sees me frown. "She loves them anyway."

In the autumn,
Grandma helps me
pick apples
to make pie.

"I like those pears,"
she says. "I must pick them for
my purse and put them
in preserves."

I giggle.
"They are apples, Grandma.
They are for our pie.
Remember?"

"No," she says with a frown.
"That's okay," I say. "I'll
remember for you."

Dad bakes her favorite
mile-high apple pie now,
and Grandma helps.
"Peel them this way."
She shows me how to take
the skin from the apple.
When I cut away the bruised parts,
Grandma stops me.

"The bruised parts are best," she says.
"All the sweetness in the apple
rushes to the soft brown part."
Dad laughs, but Grandma insists.
"I remember," she says.
"A fruit man told me once."

We keep the bruised parts in
our mile-high apple pie.
Because Grandma remembered.

Grandma likes to take Princess Pepper
for a walk. Sometimes I go with them.
Grandma remembers
lots of things—
like ice trucks
and milk wagons
and rationing.

But she can't remember the way home.
Yesterday, she went into a neighbor's house
by mistake.

Grandma's remembering is getting worse.

One day after school, Grandma is in her chair rocking **quick, quick, quick.**

She smiles at me when I come close.

"And Who are you, my dear?"

At first I think she's teasing. But then
I see that look on her face and I know.

My head
gets all
whooshy;
my eyes
start to
sting.

Grandma
can't
remember
who
I am.
I go to my room without
giving her a hug.

"Grandma's brain is all **mixed** up,"
Mom says as she rubs my back.
"But she still loves you,
even if she can't remember your name."

Now, I let Mom take Grandma for walks.
I practice the piano when she's not around.

Sometimes I wish I could
crawl into Grandma's lap
like Princess Pepper.
And other times I wish
Grandma didn't live
here anymore.

One day, Grandma leaves for a week.
"We need a break," Dad says.
Princess Pepper stays behind. She prowls
and meows and can't find a place to settle.
I have three friends over at once
and we make lots of noise.

Mom makes
spicy tacos and
pepperoni pizza, the
things Grandma hates.

But no one sits in
the special chair
and rocks

quick,
quick,
quick.

Grandma comes back on a sunny afternoon.
She sits in her chair and pats
Princess Pepper on the head.
I watch her and wonder.

Will she
know me
today?

She pulls me close.
"Hello, my dear," she says.
"Do you know who I am?" I ask.
Grandma's eyes look confused.
Finally, she laughs.
"You are my sweetness. The one who
brings me flowers and plays the piano.
You are my apple-cheeked bruise girl."

At first, I
don't understand.
But then
I smile.

I am like the
sweet parts in Grandma's
mile-high apple pie.
Her favorite food.

I push Princess Pepper
over and crawl into
Grandma's lap.

"I am
Margaret,"
I say.

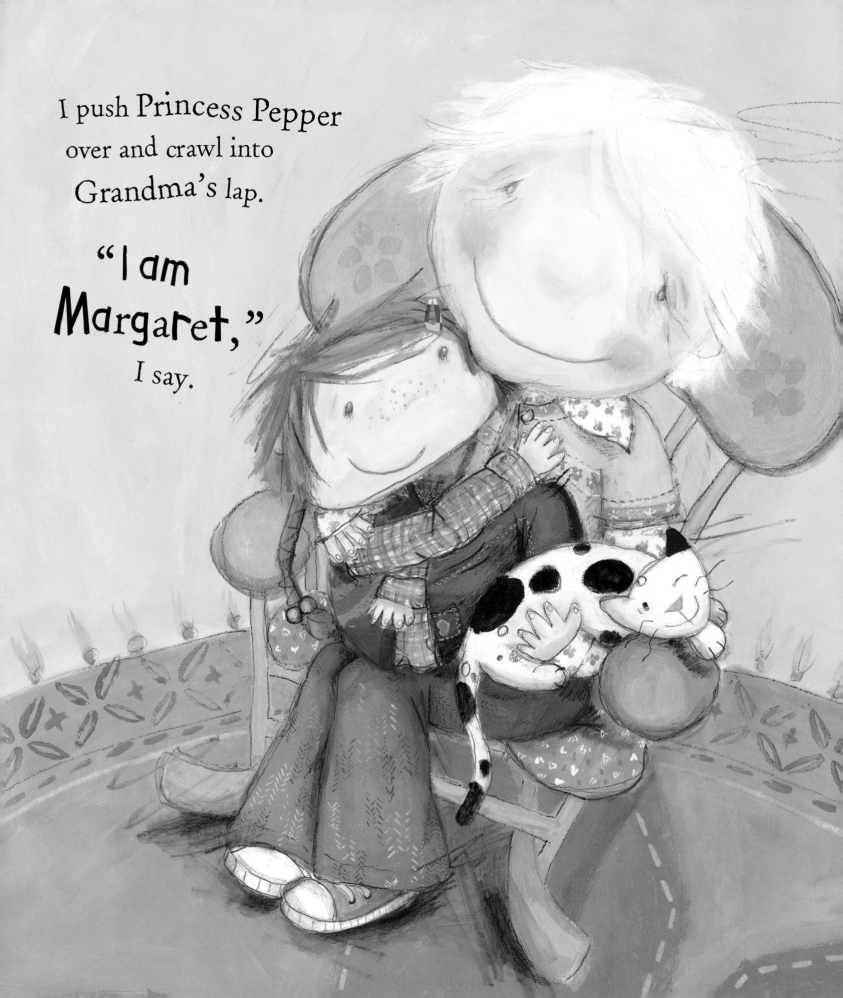

"I am your remembering."

MILE-HIGH APPLE PIE

10 Granny Smith apples

3/4 cup white sugar

3 tablespoons flour

1 teaspoon nutmeg

2–3 teaspoons cinnamon

1/4 teaspoon ground cloves

1/4 teaspoon salt

2 tablespoons butter

Prepared pie crusts for a

double-crust pie

1 egg beaten with

1 tablespoon water